J 636.088 Zei
Zeiger, Jennifer author.
Animals helping after disasters /

34028087432929
ALD $29.00 ocn885313527
04/08/15

3 4028 08743 2929
HARRIS COUNTY PUBLIC LIBRARY

W9-AJR-458

Animals Helping After Disasters

JENNIFER ZEIGER

Children's Press®
An Imprint of Scholastic Inc.
New York Toronto London Auckland Sydney
Mexico City New Delhi Hong Kong
Danbury, Connecticut

Content Consultant
Dr. Stephen S. Ditchkoff
Professor of Wildlife Sciences
Auburn University
Auburn, Alabama

Library of Congress Cataloging-in-Publication Data
Zeiger, Jennifer, author.
  Animals helping after disasters / Jennifer Zeiger.
      pages cm. — (A true book)
  Summary: "Learn how animals can be trained to help people after disasters." — Provided by
publisher.
  Audience: Ages 9–12.
  Audience: Grades 4 to 6.
  Includes bibliographical references and index.
  ISBN 978-0-531-21257-8 (library binding : alk. paper) — ISBN 978-0-531-21286-8 (pbk. : alk. paper)
  1. Rescue dogs—Juvenile literature. 2. Detector dogs—Juvenile literature. 3. Search and rescue
operations—Juvenile literature. 4. Working animals—Juvenile literature. I. Title. II. Series: True book.
  SF428.55.Z45 2015
  636.088'6—dc23   2014030582

No part of this publication may be reproduced in whole or in part, or stored in a retrieval system,
or transmitted in any form or by any means, electronic, mechanical, photocopying, recording, or
otherwise, without written permission of the publisher. For information regarding permission,
write to Scholastic Inc., Attention: Permissions Department, 557 Broadway, New York, NY 10012.

© 2015 Scholastic Inc.
All rights reserved. Published in 2015 by Children's Press, an imprint of Scholastic Inc. Published
simultaneously in Canada. Printed in China 62
SCHOLASTIC, CHILDREN'S PRESS, A TRUE BOOK™, and associated logos are trademarks and/or
registered trademarks of Scholastic Inc.
1 2 3 4 5 6 7 8 9 10 R 24 23 22 21 20 19 18 17 16 15

Front cover: A dog in a lifeguard vest
Back cover: A rescue dog on patrol in Italy

Find the Truth!

Everything you are about to read is true *except* for one of the sentences on this page.

Which one is **TRUE**?

T or F   Horses are used to track scents in forests or open areas.

T or F   Most search and rescue dog teams are paid for their time.

Find the answers in this book.

Contents

THE **BIG** TRUTH!

4

A search team explores the wreckage of the World Trade Center in New York City.

4 Disaster in the City

What makes disasters in cities so dangerous? **29**

5 Learning the Job

How are disaster response animals trained?......**35**

The golden retriever is the most common breed used in search and rescue.

Tornadoes can cause massive damage to homes and other buildings, trapping people inside.

CHAPTER 1

Search, Find, and Rescue

An earthquake collapses bridges and buildings. A tornado rips through a town. A hurricane hits the coast with heavy rains and flooding. An **avalanche** buries hikers high in the mountains. A bomb explodes in a heavily populated area. A child goes missing.

In disasters such as these, people work hard to save lives and find anyone who has gone missing. Sometimes, the help of animals can bring a mission much closer to success.

 More than 1,000 tornadoes are reported each year in the United States.

A History of Helping

Dogs are the most common animals to help out in disasters. They were first **domesticated** thousands of years ago as hunting partners. Ancient people took advantage of dogs' sharp senses of smell, sight, and hearing to find and retrieve prey. These same abilities are now used to track down people. Dogs are trained to find wartime enemies and suspected criminals. They can also search for lost or injured people after a disaster. One of the most well-known examples of this is the St. Bernard.

Ancient cave art depicts hunters working alongside dogs.

Monks relied on their St. Bernards to help find lost travelers.

A St. Bernard named Barry saved more than 40 people in the Swiss Alps between 1800 and 1812.

Monks in the Swiss Alps originally bred the St. Bernard in the 1600s. They named the new breed after their monastery's founder, St. Bernard de Menthon. The dogs helped clear snowy paths and rescue people in the Alps for centuries. They often searched in groups of two or three. If someone was found buried, the dogs dug him or her out of the snow. One dog would lie on the person for warmth while another fetched help.

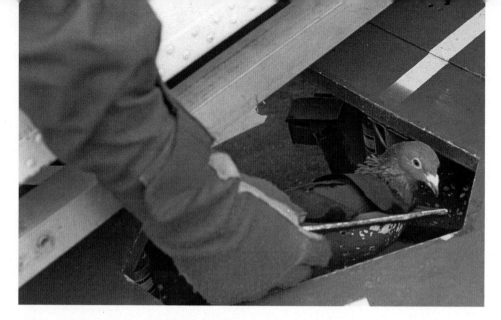

A pigeon is strapped into a coast guard helicopter.

Hunters have long relied on help from falcons. The birds' keen eyesight makes them valuable for spotting prey from the sky. In the 1970s and 1980s, researchers found that birds could be used for another type of work: search and rescue. For a short time, the U.S. Coast Guard used pigeons to spot objects, such as people or debris in the water, from a helicopter. The birds were 93 percent accurate. This was a big improvement over the 38 percent accuracy of the human crew.

Other animals have used their senses to help out humans. Theodore Roosevelt reportedly claimed that his horse helped him find bison during a hunt in the western United States. There are stories of a horse that saved its rider by sensing nearby enemies. People have also received help from rats and dolphins. Even goldfish may one day be useful to humans, by alerting us when they sense dangerous chemicals in the water.

In addition to serving as president, Theodore Roosevelt was a famed hunter and outdoorsman.

11

CHAPTER 2

Super Senses

Humans are clever. We can follow clues and solve puzzles. But our abilities are limited. This is where animals come in. They can often smell, see, and hear things that humans cannot. As a result, well-trained animals can help make a search and rescue (SAR) mission a lot more successful than humans can alone.

 Humans have about 6 million cells devoted to scent. Dogs have about 300 million.

How We Smell

All living things, including humans, produce scents. Every creature smells a little different. People may not always be able to tell each other apart by scent, but dogs, horses, and other animals can. An individual's scent depends on a number of things, including health, diet, location, habits, and **heredity**. The temperature and amount of moisture in the air also affect a person's scent.

Every person has a unique scent.

Dogs can use their powerful noses to locate things that are not within view.

Humans shed an estimated 40,000 skin cells each minute.

Picking Up the Scent

Scent is an incredibly important sense for most disaster response animals. Human scents are mostly carried by dead skin cells that we constantly shed. These skin cells, called rafts, are too small to be seen with the naked eye. However, most animals can smell them. The rafts carry odor-producing **bacteria**. A working animal can smell the bacteria on the ground or in the air and follow them to their source.

Dogs can see very well at night.

Eyes and Ears

Many searches take place in the dark or in areas covered with dense vegetation or debris. Human eyesight is very limited in these situations. However, the eyes of dogs and other SAR animals are much better suited to these situations. These animals are able to continue a search into the night. They can also peer into dark crevices and spot a person trapped beneath rubble.

Excellent hearing can be an advantage on a search, too. For example, if someone is lost, injured, or trapped and is calling for help, a dog or horse would notice this sound before humans did. The animals can also pick up on quieter sounds, such as a person's movement or breathing.

Some dogs are trained to lie down when they smell a human scent.

CHAPTER 3

Through the Wilderness

There are a variety of disasters people might face. Some of them are natural, caused by weather or activity below the earth. Others are caused by human actions. Disasters can happen anywhere, from rural areas that are miles from the nearest town to massive cities with millions of residents. Each type of disaster presents its own challenges to human and animal workers.

⬅ SAR dogs bark differently after finding a healthy person, an injured person, or a dead body.

Nose to the Ground

Sometimes a person becomes lost or goes missing. Other times, someone is kidnapped or a criminal is on the run. Depending on the situation, law enforcement and rescue workers might use tracking or trailing dogs. These dogs follow a trail wherever it goes. Tracking dogs follow a person's physical path, such as footprints. Trailing dogs focus more on the scent of rafts and other particles that a person has left behind.

Bloodhounds can pick up a trail weeks after other breeds can no longer detect it.

Sniffing the air allows dogs to follow scent trails of people who might not have touched the ground.

Nose in the Air

Some animals are trained to follow scents in the air. Rafts and other scent-carrying particles are carried by the wind and can drift out in what is called a scent plume. This irregular cone covers a narrow area near the source, widening with distance. Air-scenting dogs and horses often carefully search an area until they pick up on the scent plume. Then they follow the scent to its source.

Searching through forests requires a different set of skills than searching in a city.

Specialties

Some environments are particularly challenging to search. As a result, response animals are often trained to work in specific locations. For example, some dogs are trained to search wilderness areas, including forests and open fields. SAR horses are often used in these areas, too. Other dogs are trained for snow or water searches.

Searching the Snow

An avalanche or snow rescue dog's biggest enemy is time. Up to 90 percent of the people found within 15 minutes after an avalanche survive. That number drops to about 30 percent over the next 20 minutes. Snow is another challenge. A person could be buried under several feet of snow. Dogs search for scents that travel up to the surface. A search dog itself risks becoming buried in severe weather or another avalanche.

A dog in Austria once detected a person buried under 24 feet (7.3 meters) of snow.

Under the Water

Water searches present a different set of challenges. First, a search area can only be accessed by boat. Second, a dog must detect a body through the water by following scents that float to the surface. A third issue is water movement. **Currents**, animals, plants, and searchers disturb the water. This spreads scents around and makes it difficult to pinpoint exactly where a body is.

Water search dogs travel on boats with their handlers.

A Special Kind of Searcher

Cadaver dogs work where there are no survivors. They help search for bodies and body parts at crime scenes, after major natural disasters or **terrorist** attacks, and at water sites.

When a search and rescue dog finds a living person, the person's voice or movement is a reward for a job well done. For a cadaver dog, there is no such response when it finds a dead body. As a result, these dogs are specially trained to expect rewards from their human handlers but not from their discoveries.

Supplies

There are all kinds of equipment an animal or its handler might need on the job. Some of these supplies depend on the type of search and rescue operation being done. Others are usually carried no matter where a team is working.

Harness and Leash
Some dogs roam independently as they search. Others are kept on a leash and harness. A trailing dog might be on a leash that is 30 feet (9 m) long! This gives the dog plenty of room to work.

Emergency Supplies
First aid kits, extra food and water, flashlights, and other items are important. A handler never knows when these things might be useful.

Navigation
A SAR team should always know its own location, especially in fields, forests, mountains, and similar areas. Digital maps are handy, but teams might also bring along a good old-fashioned paper map and compass.

Climbing and Digging Gear
If a team is working in the mountains or in the snow, it might need to carry gear to travel over, under, or around obstacles.

Rewards
Animals need to know they have done their job well. When a SAR or trailing dog makes a find, its handler often gives it a favorite toy or treat.

High-Visibility Clothing
Working animals generally wear brightly colored vests that identify them as SAR or other animals on the job. Their human partners also often wear special vests or coats.

A search team explores the wreckage of the World Trade Center after the terrorist attacks of September 11, 2001.

CHAPTER 4

Disaster in the City

Search and rescue teams working in urban environments receive extra training and often **certification**. When cities are hit by a disaster, the broken remains of collapsed buildings and other structures create an unstable surface. A SAR dog needs to be careful not to slip or fall. It must also avoid sharp metal, glass, and other hazards. In addition, urban areas are densely populated. This means there are a lot of potential victims to search for and save and recover.

Many SAR dogs wear protective boots, but urban SAR dogs generally work without them for better footing.

Dogs can easily maneuver across rubble and other dangerous terrain.

Natural Disasters

Severe weather events such as tornadoes and hurricanes can cause serious damage. Earthquakes, floods, and other natural disasters can be equally destructive. People may become trapped beneath collapsed structures or inside damaged or flooded homes. Local and state SAR workers are the first to respond in these events. In especially severe disasters, teams from across the country or even the world are brought in.

Urban SAR dogs help find survivors in the initial search and rescue operations. They may also help out with cleanup afterward. Following the Gulf Coast flooding caused by Hurricane Katrina in 2005, SAR dogs scoured abandoned buildings in a final search for anyone living or dead before the buildings were demolished and the area was cleared.

Urban SAR dogs are the only SAR dogs that can be certified by the Federal Emergency Management Agency.

A dog and its handler search for survivors in New Orleans, Louisiana, after Hurricane Katrina.

Accidents and Attacks

Train wrecks, plane crashes, and other man-made accidents can also require the help of SAR animals. Terrorist attacks sometimes cause even greater devastation and loss of life than natural disasters. When these happen, SAR teams search the debris for people who are alive and in need of help. They also look for the remains of people who have died. Identifying those who died and returning them to their families help the families find closure and recover from the loss.

Dogs were an important part of the effort to find victims of the September 11 attacks.

SAR dogs might work 12- to 16-hour shifts following a major disaster.

This work is difficult and long. Animal and human rescue workers must work together to keep going. For example, SAR dogs on-site after the 1995 Oklahoma City bombing and the terrorist attacks of September 11, 2001, provided comfort to rescue workers and victims alike. So few survivors were found after these attacks that rescue workers occasionally hid in the rubble for the dogs to find. This gave the dogs the satisfaction of finally finding a living person.

During training, handlers hide in places where it will be difficult for dogs to find them.

CHAPTER 5

Learning the Job

SAR teams come from a variety of locations and backgrounds. In the United States, most SAR handlers and dogs are volunteers from all across the country. Handlers might be firefighters, police officers, or everyday **civilians**.

No matter who is on the team or where they come from, responding to a disaster is never easy. Extensive training and continuous practice are required for a dog and its handler.

Most SAR dogs train for at least a year before going on missions.

A Good Dog

A good disaster response dog can be any breed or even a mutt. However, the most common dogs used are German shepherds, Labrador and golden retrievers, border collies, and Belgian Malinois. An ideal dog for this job is strong, smart, and easy to train. It should also be **obedient**. Most importantly, the dog must have an incredibly strong drive to play and retrieve. This drive is what keeps a dog going through a long and difficult search.

Timeline of Search and Rescue Events

September 11, 2001

Terrorist attacks lead to SAR efforts in New York City, Arlington, VA, and Pennsylvania.

April 1995

SAR workers identify 168 dead and more than 500 injured people after the Alfred P. Murrah Federal Building in Oklahoma City, Oklahoma, is bombed.

Training With a Game

Training usually begins when a dog is young. Many dogs are trained as puppies. Training often starts with a simple game of hide-and-seek. First, the handler plays with the dog with a certain toy. The person runs off to hide with the toy, making sure the dog sees where he or she goes. Then the dog is let loose to find the handler and toy. Once the handler is found, he or she uses the toy to play with the dog.

February 2003

SAR teams search the rubble of the space shuttle *Columbia* after the ship is destroyed.

March 2011

Dogs from around the world take part in SAR efforts in Japan after an earthquake and tsunami.

August 2005

SAR teams and cadaver dogs search for people along the Gulf Coast after Hurricane Katrina.

By walking on nets, dogs learn how to deal with difficult terrain.

The game gradually becomes more complicated. The dog might not see where the handler hides, or the handler might hide farther away. Many dogs also begin learning how to work in certain environments. Snow SAR dogs learn how to sniff for people under the snow. Urban SAR dogs learn how to maneuver around obstacles and unstable surfaces. Trailing dogs practice picking out one person's scent from other scents.

A Good Horse

Much like a disaster response dog, a SAR horse needs to be sturdy and smart. It also needs to have a strong drive to play. It should work calmly, without being spooked by sounds, lights, people, or other horses. Because horses are most often used in searches of wide areas, a horse must be able to work slowly and steadily for a thorough search. During training, horses are taught to follow scents, stay calm, and trust their riders.

Rescue horses are trained to walk on a variety of surfaces.

Handlers must learn how to give orders to and cooperate with their animals.

Human Training

A disaster response animal's human partner also goes through training. SAR people should be physically fit and willing to work in almost any kind of weather. They must be able to navigate in a variety of ways, including with a map and compass. They also need to know first aid and some basic survival techniques in case they need to help a victim, their animal, or themselves.

Communication

Communication is extremely important to a SAR team. People working with SAR horses are experts at reading a horse's body language. Dogs and their handlers learn commands. "Find it" is a dog's cue to search. If the dog becomes distracted, its handler might say "Leave it." "Tunnel" and "Over" help a dog get around obstacles. When a dog makes a find, it either barks to call its handler over or runs to fetch the person. When fetched, a handler will often tell the dog, "Show me."

A Job Well Done

When it is time to retire, some disaster response animals take on easier jobs. Dogs might work as **therapy** animals. Urban SAR dogs sometimes switch to less demanding forms of SAR, such as wilderness searches. Some disaster response dogs become a member of their handlers' families or are adopted by other people. SAR horses often take up a restful life on a farm.

Many rescue dogs, such as this German shepherd who helped recover victims of the September 11 attacks, find homes with loving families after they retire.

New technology will help make rescue dogs more effective than ever before.

The Future of Disaster Response

Each disaster presents new challenges and new learning experiences. Researchers are beginning to experiment with ways to enhance tracking and SAR efforts. Horses and even mules could play larger roles in SAR operations. Perhaps one day, every SAR dog will have a camera so human rescuers can see what the dogs see. As humans and animals continue to work together, disaster response can continue to become better and better. ★

Average number of years a SAR dog trains before going on missions: 1

Number of years a dog usually trains before earning urban SAR certification by the U.S. government: 2 or more

Number of urban SAR dog and handler teams with advanced U.S. government certification: 150

Number of dogs involved in search and rescue after the terrorist attacks of September 11, 2001: Almost 300

Number of lives saved by St. Bernards in St. Bernard Pass in the Swiss Alps: More than 2,000 documented people

Did you find the truth?

T Horses are used to track scents in forests or open areas.

F Most search and rescue dog teams are paid for their time.

Resources

Books

Bozzo, Linda. *Search and Rescue Dog Heroes*. Berkeley Heights, NJ: Enslow, 2011.

Laughlin, Kara L. *Search-and-Rescue Dogs*. Mankato, MN: The Child's World, 2014.

Patent, Dorothy Hinshaw. *Super Sniffers: Dog Detectives on the Job*. New York: Bloomsbury, 2014.

Visit this Scholastic Web site for more information on animals helping after disasters:

★ www.factsfornow.scholastic.com

Enter the keywords **Animals Helping After Disasters**

Important Words

avalanche (AV-uh-lanch) — a large mass of snow, ice, or earth that suddenly falls down the side of a mountain

bacteria (bak-TEER-ee-uh) — microscopic, single-celled living things that exist everywhere and can be either useful or harmful

cadaver (kuh-DAV-ur) — dead body

certification (sur-ti-fi-KAY-shun) — official recognition of an ability to perform a certain task

civilians (suh-VIL-yunz) — people who are not members of the armed forces or police forces

currents (KUR-uhnts) — movements of water in a definite direction in a river or an ocean

domesticated (duh-MES-ti-kay-tid) — a domesticated animal has been tamed so it can live with or be used by people

heredity (huh-RED-i-ty) — physical and mental qualities passed from a parent to a child before the child is born

obedient (oh-BEE-dee-uhnt) — willing to follow orders

terrorist (TER-ur-ist) — someone who uses violence or threats in order to, for example, frighten people, obtain power, or force a government to do something

therapy (THER-uh-pee) a treatment for an illness, injury, disability, or psychological problem

Index

Page numbers in **bold** indicate illustrations.

About the Author

Jennifer Zeiger lives in Chicago, Illinois, where she writes and edits books for children.

PHOTOGRAPHS ©: 123RF/Dani Simmonds: 26 top; age fotostock: 40 (G Kopp), 41 (McPHOTO); Alamy Images: 18 (blickwinkel), 15 (Graham M. Lawrence); AP Images: 25 (Dave Martin), 5 bottom, 33 (Mark Humphrey), cover (Rex Features); FEMA: 5 top, 28, 36 (Andrea Booher), 16, 22, 31, 37 (Jocelyn Augustino), 32 (Mike Rieger); Getty Images: 42 (Charlotte Dumas/Barcroft USA), 30 (Joe Raedle), 24 (Matt Cardy), 11 (T W Ingersoll/MPI), back cover (Tiziana Fabi/Stringer); Landov: 39, 44 (Matt Stamey/Gainesville Sun), 3, 12 (Nacho Doce/Reuters); Media Bakery/Emmerichwebb: 14; Newscom: 34 (Brian Cahn/ZUMA Press), 17 (David Eulitt/MCT), 20 (Marty Bicek/ ZUMAPRESS), 38 (O Diez/picture alliance/Arco Images G); REX USA: 4, 27 bottom right (FLPA), 21 (Global Warming Images), 43 (HFRS/Solent News), 27 center (Nils Jorgensen); Shutterstock, Inc.: 26 bottom (drohn), 27 top (Mike Flippo), 23 (Nikolai Tsvetkov), 27 bottom left (Richard Peterson), Superstock, Inc.: 8 (Fred Hirschmann), 9 (Image Asset Management Ltd.); Thinkstock: 6 (gabes1976); U.S. Coast Guard: 10.

Harris County Public Library, Houston, TX